My Journey Through Art

CREATE YOUR OWN MASTERPIECES

Text by Kathryn Cave

Illustrations by Melvin Bramich

BARRON'S

In Association With the

National Gallery of Art, Washington, D.C.

First edition for the United States, the Philippines, and Canada published 1994 by Barron's Educational Series, Inc.
First published under the title *Create your own Masterpiece* © Frances Lincoln Limited 1994
Drawings by Melvin Bramich

First published in Great Britain in 1994 by
Frances Lincoln Limited, 4 Torriano Mews
Torriano Avenue, London NW5 2RZ

All inquiries should be addressed to:
Barron's Educational Series, Inc.
250 Wireless Boulevard
Hauppauge, NY 11788

International Standard Book No. 0-8120-1924-5

Printed and bound in Italy
4567 9870 987654321

Would you like to create your own masterpieces?
As you take a journey through this book, every page gives
you the opportunity to make your own work of art.

Before you start, you'll need to pack essentials for the voyage—
paints, pencils, crayons, felt-tip markers, scissors,
glue—and of course, this book. Then zoom off
at the wheel of your car to meet adventure,
excitement, and perhaps even danger on a
fast-moving artistic journey through art. You can set sail to
a mysterious island, go riding on a ranch, or camp out in the desert—
you'll find something new to do, and draw, around every corner.

Every time you turn the page, the story takes a new twist.
The notes and picture outlines give you suggestions about
what to draw, but it's up to you to fill in the details of your
adventures, using paints, pens, cut-outs, or anything else
you can think of to make your book look as colorful
and exciting as possible.

Each of the stops on the way is based on an image from a
painting in the National Gallery of Art, in Washington, D.C.
You can see the paintings if you visit the gallery, but there is
also a small picture of each one inside the back cover.

So, pack your paint box, and get ready to go.
Turn the pages—and have a good trip!

Remember me!

You're leaving home to see the world! Before you go, you ask your favorite artist to paint your portrait. You give the picture to your family to remember you by.

- Fill the frame with the portrait your artist paints.
- Write your name in the space at the bottom of the frame—or make up a new name for yourself and write that there instead!

If you want some ideas, you could look at the paintings by Rembrandt Peale, Amedeo Modigliani, and Mary Cassatt reproduced inside the back cover.

Pack a picnic

It's your last night at home, and you plan to set out first thing in the morning. Before you go to bed, you go down to the kitchen and pack a delicious picnic lunch to take with you on the journey. You put in lots of fruit and—what else?

• Draw in the rest of the kitchen table and all the things you are going to pack to eat and drink on your picnic.
• Underneath the table there is something you *really* don't want to forget—you never travel without it. Show what it is in your picture.

The fruit comes from a painting by Paul Cézanne called *Still Life with Apples and Peaches*. You can see the whole painting inside the back cover.

Goodbye!

You're off at last! Who knows what lies ahead—excitement, adventure, danger? You can't wait to find out. All the same, halfway down the road you turn and look back through the gateway.

- Draw the view you see of the home you are leaving behind.
- Someone is waving goodbye from a window. Put them in your picture, too.

The road and gateway come from a painting by Vincent van Gogh called *Farmhouse in Provence, Arles*. You'll find it inside the back cover. There is also a painting by Edward Hopper that might give you some ideas.

By the roadside

You pick up your car and drive all morning. Suddenly you see the ideal place to stop for lunch. You pull off the road and enjoy your picnic. Then you go for a walk and see wonderful plants and butterflies.

- Fill the empty pages of your book with drawings and paintings of the fantastic plants you see in the picnic area.

- The butterflies have the most brilliant colors you have ever seen, and each one is different. Show them resting or fluttering around the plants in your picture.

The plants and butterfly are from *A Bouquet of Flowers with Insects* by Pierre Joseph Redouté. You'll find it in color inside the back cover.

Cartoon time

The person who last stayed in your
hotel room left a newspaper behind.
When you see the cartoon on the front
page, you burst out laughing.

- Draw in the rest of the cartoon as
you imagine it.
- Give the characters speech bubbles
so that we can all share the joke. Write
the words first. Then draw bubbles
around the words.

The characters are from a cartoon by the
French artist Honoré Daumier. You can
read the translation of his original caption
below the cartoon inside the back cover.

Breakdown

Your car made odd noises all morning,
and now it has broken down outside
a strange farm, miles from nowhere.
Luckily the farmer has a telephone,
so you can call the repair truck.
While you wait for the truck to
arrive...

● Draw what you can see of the farm:
house, barn, animals—everything.
● Color your drawing in with the
brightest felt-tip pens you can find.

This is part of Joan Miró's painting *The Farm*.
The whole painting is reproduced inside
the back cover.

Dawn in the desert

You take a wrong turn late at night and never reach your hotel. You find a dry cave and settle down in your sleeping bag for the night. Next morning, you wake up at sunrise to discover you are not alone!

● Draw or paint whatever or whomever you find sharing your cave.

● Show the spectacular view of the desert you can see framed in the rocky cave mouth.

The cave is from Giovanni Bellini's *Saint Jerome Reading*. If you find the painting inside the back cover, you'll be able to compare your view of the landscape with his.

Riding into trouble

You need a break from driving, so
you stop at a ranch to go riding instead.
It's lucky for you that you're a skilled
rider, because you run into something
unexpected.

- Draw or paint yourself on the horse.
- Something or someone has given
your horse a dreadful fright—show
what it is in your picture.

Saint George was the original rider of this
horse, in Raphael's painting *Saint George
and the Dragon*. You'll find the painting
reproduced inside the back cover.

Undiscovered country

The road you've been following ends at the water's edge. You leave your car and journey on by boat. Just over the horizon is an island that isn't on any map.

● Draw or paint what the island looks like from near the shore.

● While you are gazing at the island, you are surprised to see a strange boat sailing in your direction. Where does it come from and who can be in it? Add the boat to your picture.

Your boat is from Fitz Hugh Lane's *Lumber Schooners at Evening on Penobscot Bay*. You can find the painting inside the back cover.

Gold coins

The inhabitants of the island have strange and wonderful designs on their coins. You're so impressed by them that you copy four of the designs into your book.

● Fill in the blank coins opposite with designs and mottoes of your own.

● Your brand new coins are for a brand new country. Invent a name for it and write it underneath your coin designs.

The coin designs on this page are from etchings by Jaques Callot. There are more inside the back cover.

Sea monsters

A storm blows in when you're on the boat again, and it's too rough to draw or paint. Luckily you have scissors and a glue stick with you, and there's a box of old magazines and postcards in your cabin, so you have everything you need to make a collage of all the creatures of the sea.

● Make lots of cut-out sea creatures: jellyfish, octopuses, eels, sharks, whales, and fish of every shape and color—and glue them onto the opposite page.

● Cut out wavy strips of paper to make seaweed for your underwater world and glue them onto your collage.

The designs opposite come from a collage by Henri Matisse, *Beasts of the Sea*. You can see the whole collage inside the back cover.

A sailor's story

The boat sails on, and on, and on.... The days seem endless, and you've read all your books twice already. You spend the afternoons listening to stories the crew tell of adventures they've had at sea. One of the stories is so vivid you can almost see it happening.

● Part of the story is shown on the opposite page. Fill in the rest of the details to show what is going on.

The people in this boat come from a painting by John Singleton Copley called *Watson and the Shark*. If you want to see the rest of the story, look for the painting inside the back cover.

Landfall!

You can see land at last. You can't
wait to get your feet onto dry
ground again. As soon as you've found
a place to stay, you go off for a stroll
around town.

• Paint in the buildings you can see
around the harbor, using a small
paintbrush and applying color in
dots like the rest of the picture.

• It's a wonderful day: the sky is blue
and the water shimmers in the bright
sunlight. Use bigger blobs of color
to paint in the sea and the sky in
your picture.

The lighthouse is from Georges Seurat's
The Lighthouse at Honfleur. It is reproduced
inside the back cover.

Evening

You're back on the road again—but
it feels like the road to nowhere.
At sunset, you finally come to a house
and stop to ask for directions.

● What does the lonely house look
like? Draw in the rest of the house—
walls, windows, roof, shutters, and all.
● What is the man looking at? Draw it
in your picture.

The doorway and the man are from Edward
Hopper's *Cape Cod Evening*. To see what else
the artist put in the painting, look inside
the back cover.

Across the bridge

You're back on the right track, and you've found a great place to stay, overlooking a river. You can see several boats from your window, and a bridge, and a town on the other side of the water.

- Draw or paint the bridge and the buildings on the far shore.
- Make some more sailboats from scraps of paper and glue them onto your picture.

The boat is from Claude Monet's *The Bridge at Argenteuil*. It is reproduced inside the back cover.

Strange birds

Walking deep in the forest, you see some birds you recognize—and some you don't!

● Fill these torn-out pages from your notebook with sketches of the strange and colorful birds you see.

● Invent a name for each bird, and write it underneath the picture.

The bird on this page and *Cardinal Grosbeak* opposite were painted by John James Audubon. You'll find them both inside the back cover.

CARDINAL GROSBEAK

Wheels

You're out exploring the streets of a new town one quiet evening when you hear the sound of wheels. You barely have time to jump out of the way before a group of cyclists sweeps past with a crowd of people and vehicles following.

● Draw or paint the other road-users you see streaming past.

The bicyclists come from Lyonel Feininger's *The Bicycle Race*, reproduced inside the back cover.

Winter's kingdom

It's winter here, although your family and friends back home are still enjoying the sun.

- Add some more wintry-looking trees and buildings to this picture of the view from your hotel room.
- Before you've finished the picture, it starts to snow again. Tear some white paper into small pieces and stick them over your picture to look like snowflakes.

This scene comes from *Skating Scene* by John Toole. You'll find it inside the back cover.

An afternoon snack

After a day of fun in the snow, you feel really hungry. Hurrying back to your hotel, you pass a bakery. Its window display is the most tempting you have ever seen....

● Fill the spaces with pictures of the delicious-looking cakes and cookies you see in the window.

● You can see the shopkeeper through the window too. Show him standing behind the cakes.

The cakes are from Wayne Thiebaud's *Cakes*, reproduced inside the back cover.

Amazing art

The last city you visit has a marvelous
art gallery with lots of exciting
modern paintings.

● Fill the space on the opposite page
with squiggles, swirls, straight lines,
blobs, splashes, cut-outs—whatever
you like—to create a wild and
wonderful abstract painting all
your own.

● When you've finished, make an
unusual frame for your painting.

If you need a little inspiration, you might like
to look at the paintings by Jackson Pollock and
Juan Gris, inside the back cover.

City skyline

It's time to head for home at last.
As your train pulls out of the station,
you get a wonderful view of the bright
city skyline through the window.

● Fill in the rest of the skyline.
There could be spires, turrets, domes,
whatever you like!
● What else can you can see from
the train? Shops? Houses? Churches?
Statues? Factories? Show them all in
your picture.

The buildings on the opposite page come
from a painting by Auguste Renoir, called
Pont Neuf, Paris. You can find it inside the flap
on the back cover.

Welcome home

Your train pulls into your station, and you can't wait to see your family and friends again. As you walk toward the grand station exit, you catch sight of them waiting outside.

● Draw or paint the people you love—waving, calling, cheering—happy to welcome you home!

This imposing archway was never actually built! Jan van der Heyden painted it as part of *An Architectural Fantasy*, reproduced inside the back cover.

Jaques Callot (1592 - 1635)

The Coins 1662

Henri Matisse (1869 - 1954)

Beasts of the Sea 1950

Lyonel Feininger (1871 - 1956)

The Bicycle Race 1912

Honoré Daumier (1808 - 1879)

It is rather flattering to have so many pupils!... 1838

Joan Miró (1893 - 1983)

The Farm 1921 - 1922

Jackson Pollock (1912 - 1956)

Number 1, 1950 (Lavender Mist) 1950